Playing Possum

Playing Possum

Jennifer Black Reinhardt

Clarion Books
Houghton Mifflin Harcourt
Boston   New York

Alfred was born a possum.
And when a possum feels nervous,
it freezes and plays dead.

This was unfortunate for Alfred.
He was a very nervous possum.

Because of his nervous nature, Alfred felt uncomfortable being the focus of attention. Any attention.

So he did not do well at school.

He did not excel at sports.

And making friends was too terrifying to contemplate.

Alfred was a very lonely possum.

One day Alfred noticed Sofia.
Sofia was born an armadillo.
And when an armadillo feels nervous
it curls into a ball.

Meeting someone new can be scary. . . .

So Alfred played dead,

and Sofia curled up.

After a little while, they both felt calmer.
Alfred unfroze and Sofia unfurled.

And as they stared at each other, they realized they had something in common.

When they were together,
knowing this made them feel safe.

When Sofia curled up, Alfred just waited.

When Alfred froze, Sofia just waited.

They began to trust that when they became themselves again, they would see a friend.

Alfred hardly ever froze,
and Sofia was rarely round.

They saw they had something
in common with others who
sometimes felt afraid.

"We can show them kindness
and friendship," said Alfred.

"And that will make them less
anxious!" cheered Sofia.

It took some patience,

a lot of understanding,

and a little forgiveness.

But before long, making friends became easier, and so did other scary things.

And this was fortunate . . .

. . . for everyone.

A note from the author:
Truth and Imagination

It is true that many creatures in the animal kingdom display odd, unusual, funny, sometimes deadly defense mechanisms—behavior designed to discourage or disable enemies.

I have taken a few liberties in the story of Alfred and Sofia. To begin with, opossums (the formal term for possums) and armadillos are both nocturnal. They sleep during the day and are awake at night. Realistically, the whole story would have taken place in the dark.

Also, the animals pictured in the book are from all over the world, and most of them probably wouldn't hang out together in real life.

Further, defense mechanisms are instinctual—built in. I've imagined that if the animals in *Playing Possum* were to show one another empathy and understanding, their behaviors could be changed. This isn't true in real life; wild animals can't control their behavior. But people can, and sharing kindness and patience can change things for the better.

It's not true that these animals routinely wear hats and bathing suits, but a chipmunk would look dapper in a bow tie.

On the next few pages, I have listed some true things about some of the animals featured in this tale. I didn't want to draw anything gross, so I did not choose creatures that shoot blood or shed appendages. But if you're so inclined, I encourage you to research further. Your school or local library is a great place to begin.

Glossary

Armadillo: The three-banded armadillo is the only armadillo species that rolls itself into a tight, armored ball when it feels threatened.

Chameleon: When it feels anxious, a chameleon changes color to blend in to its environment and "disappear."

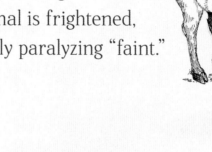

Fainting goat (Myotonic goat): This goat's muscles get stiff when the animal is frightened, causing it to fall over in a briefly paralyzing "faint."

Hedgehog: If a hedgehog feels afraid, it rolls its prickly body into a tight ball.

Octopus: When it's scared, an octopus releases dark ink from sacs located between its gills, concealing itself from foes. (Squid do this too.)

Opossum (informally, Possum): When it feels nervous or threatened, an opossum will freeze and play dead, or "play possum." It can stay in this paralyzed pose for hours.

Porcupine: When a porcupine is alarmed, it puffs out its long, sharp quills to appear larger and less vulnerable. The pointy needles detach very easily, stabbing into the unfortunate victim.

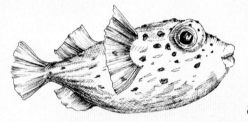

Puffer fish (Blowfish): This fish quickly gulps in water or air when it feels alarmed and inflates itself into a spiny ball.

Skunk: A frightened skunk will shoot a horribly smelly substance from a gland underneath its tail. The stench is so powerful that it can last for days.

Tortoise: The tortoise has extremely strong neck muscles. When it feels nervous it can pull its head entirely into its shell.

Dedicated with love to Joe, who makes me feel safe
—J.B.R.

CLARION BOOKS

3 Park Avenue, New York, New York 10016

Copyright © 2020 by Jennifer Black Reinhardt

Clarion Books is an imprint of
Houghton Mifflin Harcourt Publishing Company.

hmhbooks.com

The illustrations in this book were done in watercolor, ink, colored pencil, and collage,
on 300lb Lanaquarelle hot press watercolor paper.
The text was set in Fnord.

Library of Congress Cataloging-in-Publication Data
Names: Reinhardt, Jennifer Black, 1963– author, illustrator.
Title: Playing possum / Jennifer Black Reinhardt.
Description: Boston ; New York : Clarion Books, Houghton Mifflin Harcourt, [2020]
Summary: Possums play dead when threatened so Alfred, an unusually nervous possum,
avoids attention and even friendship until he meets Sofia, an armadillo who curls into a ball
when nervous. Includes facts about the unusual defense mechanisms of animals pictured in the book.
Identifiers: LCCN 2019007335 | ISBN 9781328782700 (hardcover picture book)
Subjects: | CYAC: Anxiety—Fiction. | Friendship—Fiction. | Individuality—Fiction. | Opossums—Fiction.
Armadillos—Fiction. | Classification: LCC PZ7.R276 Pl 2020 | DDC [E]—dc23
LC record available at https://lccn.loc.gov/2019007335

Manufactured in China
SCP 10 9 8 7 6 5 4 3 2 1
4500795542